For Alexandre, with the wish that he

will always fulfil his dreams. N.G.

For my sister Julie and her three clever bunnies,

Bertie, Fred & Elsie. G.T.

# A Colourful Wish

Noel Grammont ❀ Gillian Tyler

One spring morning the rays of the warm sun tickled the whiskers of a sleepy rabbit called Pipkin.

He opened one eye and saw blues and pinks striping the sky. Then he opened the other eye and saw golds and greens covering the ground around him.

"What a beautiful morning," he thought to himself.

"If only I could ..." Could what? Pipkin wasn't sure, but he had the feeling that he should do something special, and it made him restless.

His tummy growled. "Perhaps I need to eat. Some bright orange carrots would do nicely," he said to himself.

He splashed dew over his face, shook bits of grass from his fur and hop-hop-hopped along to the nearest garden. It belonged to an old artist, and today it was sparkling in the morning light.

Pipkin could see feathery carrot-tops and young cabbages, crunchy greens and sweet baby lettuces. His mouth watered. In he went.

"Good morning, Feather," Pipkin called out to a pretty white hen who was in amongst the strawberry plants, scratching and scraping for her breakfast.

"Good morning, Pipkin," replied Feather happily.

Pipkin scampered to the vegetable patch, pulled up the biggest carrot he could find and began to nibble. Then, out of the corner of his eye, he noticed somebody sitting on a stool by the blossom-covered tree.

"Look, Feather. It's the old artist," he said.

"It's strange that he never notices me coming and going, even when I take one of his crunchy carrots or his tasty cabbages."

"That's because he is concentrating," answered Feather.

$S$oon Pipkin had munched up so much that his tummy was full.

Then he began to explore, scampering under the bright pink and deep red spring flowers that hung over the garden path.

"What a beautiful garden," he thought to himself.

"If only I could ..."

$C$ould what? Pipkin wasn't sure. He still had the feeling that he should do something special, and it made him restless.

"I wonder what the old artist is doing?" he thought.

So ... very quietly ... he crept nearer and nearer, and what he saw made his whiskers quiver with excitement.

The old artist held a round board in one hand.

On it there were bright blobs of paint arranged in a circle. In his other hand he held a brush with a furry tip.

"That's as furry as my very own tail," thought Pipkin.

He watched as the artist dipped the brush into a deep red blob and then dabbed the glowing colour onto his painting.

As Pipkin looked more closely at the picture, he recognized the path and the spring flowers.

"That's the old artist's very own garden!" he gasped.

"How beautiful," he thought to himself.

"If only I could ..." Could what? At last he knew.

"If only I could do that, too!" he cried.

As Pipkin looked longingly at the artist's picture, a voice called from the nearby cottage and the old man stopped his work. He put his floppy hat on the stool and went indoors, leaving everything exactly as it was ...

The moment the artist was out of sight, Pipkin hop-hop-hopped over to the stool and slipped on the big floppy hat.

"It's sometimes possible to make dreams come true. That's what makes life so interesting," he thought excitedly, quite surprising himself.

He had never had such an important thought before. Perhaps the hat was full of the old man's thinking? Pipkin peeked out from under the brim and felt like a true artist.

Feather watched with approval.

"You know, all our old artist's work is wonderful," she said.

"He sees the world differently than others. He sees it with his heart.  People all over the world know him."

Pipkin sighed deeply.  Other rabbits only thought about food and water, but now that he had the old man's hat on, he too would be different.

"How I would love to be an artist.  That would be my dream come true. I would paint the most beautiful carrots ever seen," he cried.

For a moment he imagined how famous he would be, and how all the other rabbits would admire him.

"Why don't you start to paint now, this very moment?" Feather encouraged him. "If it's your dream, then try it."

"But it looks so difficult," sighed Pipkin.

"I t will be impossible if you don't dare to begin," replied Feather.

"But ... but ... what should I paint on?" squeaked Pipkin.

"Take some of my eggs," suggested Feather.

"There's a basket full of them under the tree. Just look how perfectly white and smooth they are," she added proudly.

Pipkin nodded in agreement.

"So, little rabbit, you must start painting right away," insisted Feather, "because there could very well be a great artist inside you."

Pipkin scampered over to get the basket of eggs. Then he carefully picked up a brush, dipped it into the purple colour and painted a wiggly line on the largest egg.

Pipkin's whiskers shook with happiness. The little rabbit no longer felt the slightest bit restless. He felt only joy as he painted egg after egg with colourful patterns. He didn't even stop when the fireflies started to glimmer in the evening shadows and Feather went home to roost for the night.

He carried on until, quite suddenly, a voice broke into the silence.

"Hmmm ... You have talent, little one."

Pipkin looked up, straight into the old artist's sea green eyes.

"Painting eggs ... What a lovely idea," said the kind old man. He picked them up one by one and looked at them closely.

"You are truly an artist," he smiled. "But, if you don't mind me saying so, it would be better if these eggs were cooked. Come tomorrow and I will cook you some eggs for painting."

Pipkin backed away shyly and tripped over the brim of the big floppy hat that was still on his head. He swept it off and scampered away, as fast as he could.

The very next day, Pipkin crept back to the garden. Sure enough, the old artist was there, his eyes twinkling. He presented Pipkin with a basketful of cooked eggs.

"And here is something else," he said, and he handed Pipkin a small floppy hat, just like his own. It fitted perfectly.

Pipkin painted some of the eggs with stripes and some with dots and squiggles. He even painted some with orange carrots good enough to eat. Then he put his masterpieces out to dry all around the garden.

He felt as happy as a rabbit could possibly be.

The next morning, the old man's grandchildren came to visit for Easter. He told them to search outside in the garden for some small but perfect treasures they could eat.

When they found the little works of art, they laughed and clapped their hands with excitement. Pipkin didn't mind them eating the eggs because he knew he could make lots more.

From that day on, Pipkin became an artist.

Feather took great pleasure in laying eggs for him, and as the story goes, Pipkin is still painting in the old man's garden.

Perhaps this is how the tradition of painting eggs began. I do not know. But what's more important is that a little rabbit is living out his dream every day!

First published in Great Britain in 2013

by

Far Far Away Books and Media Ltd.

20-22 Bedford Row, London WC1R 4JS

FAR
FAR
AWAY
BOOKS

ISBN: 978-1-908786-79-1 hardback

ISBN: 978-1-908786-35-7 paperback

A CIP catalogue record for this book is available from the British Library.

Designed at www.aitchcreative.co.uk

Printed and bound in Portugal by Printer Portuguesa

All Far Far Away Books can be ordered from

www.centralbooks.com

www.farfarawaybooks.com